T0020529

NEVER GOING BACK

SAM WIEBE

ORCA BOOK PUBLISHERS

Published in Canada and the United States in 2020 by Orca Book Publishers.
orcabook.com

Library and Archives Canada Cataloguing in Publication
Title: Never going back / Sam Wiebe.
Names: Wiebe, Sam, author.
Series: Rapid reads.
Description: Series statement: Rapid reads
Identifiers: Canadiana (print) 20200177028 | Canadiana (ebook) 20200177044 |
ISBN 9781459825772 (softcover) | ISBN 9781459825789 (PDF) |
ISBN 9781459825796 (EPUB)
Classification: LCC PS8645.I3236 N48 2020 | DDC C813/.6—dc23

Library of Congress Control Number: 2020930590

Summary: In this work of crime fiction, retired thief Ali is forced to do one more
job for her old boss to protect her younger brother and the family business.

Orca Book Publishers is committed to reducing the consumption
of nonrenewable resources in the making of our books. We make
every effort to use materials that support a sustainable future.

Orca Book Publishers gratefully acknowledges the support for its publishing
programs provided by the following agencies: the Government of Canada,
the Canada Council for the Arts and the Province of British Columbia
through the BC Arts Council and the Book Publishing Tax Credit.

Design by Ella Collier
Cover photography by Shutterstock.com/Olesia Bilkei

Printed and bound in Canada.

23 22 21 20 • 1 2 3 4

For Carly

ONE

DON'T BELIEVE WHAT you hear about me.

I don't rob people. Robbery means taking something with force. I hate violence, and I've never used a weapon in my life. Besides, I'm too good to need force. If I take something of yours, you won't know until it's gone, and you'll never know it was me.

I'm a thief. A great thief. Or I was.

But right now I was a woman waiting in the rain for her brother.

◆

Dean and I pretty much raised ourselves. After our parents' funeral, we went to live with our aunt Jessie. She owned a bar and restaurant with a small apartment on the second floor. The place is called Kidd's. Dean runs it nowadays and still lives upstairs.

My brother has always been interested in the restaurant business. I think that's because to him Kidd's is home. Dean loves to cook. Tonight, for my first meal after getting out of prison, he promised to make me something called cassoulet. I told him a burger and fries would be all right. But like I said, he loves to cook.

Me, I'm good at other things.

For two summers Aunt Jessie had a boyfriend named Paul. He installed alarms for a security company. Houses mostly. Some businesses and office buildings. I helped him with his tools, and he taught me about the security business.

When a company installs a house alarm, they let the homeowner set the code. But things go wrong. Homeowners forget. For that reason the company sets its own code too, in case of emergencies. Installers like Paul are supposed to pick a unique or random set of four numbers—7093 or 2851. Something like that. They enter this code in their computer so the office has it on file if the owners ever need it.

But installers have bad days too. Some are lazy. Paul liked to get home early, so he would always set the same code. Four zeros.

I was fifteen when I learned this. For a fifteen-year-old, that was a lot of knowledge. Half the houses in our neighborhood had stickers in the window from Paul's security company. They had the same alarm code. All I had to do was find an open window and I could be inside.

Sometimes I didn't even need an open window. Paul showed me a little about locksmithing. Not lock*picking*—that was illegal. He showed me how to use a tension tool and a lock pick, but said they should only be used if somebody got locked out.

I would practice after school. Or instead of school. Working with Paul *was* my school.

At that time I didn't want to take things. I just liked the challenge of getting into places. I wanted to open any door, defeat any alarm, know every code. That was my fantasy.

Being a thief means mastering a lot of skills. I learned to climb by practicing on empty buildings around town. When I was eighteen I worked part-time at a gym that had a rock-climbing wall. After cleaning the floors and emptying the trash, I'd practice climbing, building strength and confidence. Soon I could almost walk up walls.

>◆<

The first building I broke into on my own was my high school. But not to steal anything. To get something back for my brother.

Dean was always tall and heavy for his age. Other kids liked to bully him. They called him Big Guy or Heavy D. If he fought back, the teachers would get mad at him. He was bigger, so he should *act* bigger.

At lunch one day there was a fight on the baseball diamond. Two kids had knocked Dean down. A bat was being swung. Dean fought back, and just when he stood up and threw a punch, the lunch monitor spotted him.

Dean was sent to the principal's office.

Principal Rattigan didn't want to hear Dean's side of the story. She took his baseball glove as punishment.

That glove was a present from our dad. Dean slept with it on the pillow next to him. He loved it. He asked her to take anything else, but the principal wouldn't give it back.

Dean and I are close. I knew how upset he was without the glove. After school, when we had finished cleaning up the kitchen, I told him I would get it back for him.

"How?" he asked. "It's locked in her office. It's impossible."

"Maybe for you," I said.

The principal's office was on the second floor of the school. Her window looked down on the sports field. There were no trees nearby and nowhere to throw a rope. The doors of the school were all alarmed.

At the back of the school, near the basketball courts, was a toolshed. It took me ten minutes to pick the padlock. Inside I found a ladder that would reach to the second floor.

Up I went.

The principal's window was closed, but I worked a screwdriver between the frame and the sill and pried up the window. After stepping into the room, I searched the desk until I found Dean's glove. It was in the bottom drawer, with some other things the principal had collected from students.

I took the glove and climbed out the window. Closed it. Climbed down. I put the ladder back in the shed, locked it up and went home to surprise my brother.

I got away with it. Almost.

Dean couldn't help telling his friends what his big sister had done. Word began to get around the school. The principal called me to her office two days later.

"I hear you're quite the little thief," Principal Rattigan said.

"No, ma'am."

"No good will come of that, Alison. Admit what you did. Your fingerprints are all over my office."

I confessed. Later I would learn that she had made it up. Police don't take fingerprints for a small crime like that. I got a month of detention and learned two lessons:

1. Always wear gloves.

2. Don't trust someone just because they're bigger than you.

My detention went by slowly, but it wasn't boring. Word of my abilities had gotten around to the older kids at school. I was about to meet the person who would change my life.

Lisa Wan was two years older than me. Already she had a reputation in the neighborhood. Lisa was tough, she was wealthy, and she did exactly what she wanted. She'd never been in trouble at school. That was partly because she didn't attend class most of the time. And partly because not many teachers wanted to get on Lisa's bad side. Even Principal Rattigan was afraid to step in. At least, that was the rumor.

In detention Lisa sat on top of her desk, facing away from the blackboard. The teacher who was supposed to watch us was pretending to read a magazine.

"You're the kid who broke into Rattigan's office?" Lisa asked. "You must have found a lot of nice stuff."

"Just a glove," I said, a little nervous. "I only wanted to help my brother."

"Next time," Lisa said, "here's what you do. Bring another glove. One your brother doesn't care about. Switch it for his. You think Rattigan would notice? Do it that way and you'll never get caught."

I had to admit it was a smart idea.

"Most people only own things to own them," Lisa said. "What do they care? A smart person can make money buying and selling if they know the real value of things."

"Like what?" I asked.

"Like anything."

Lisa and I hung out together long after detention was over. Me, her and Monster. Monster was bigger and taller than Dean. I didn't know if he was Lisa's boyfriend or if he just worked for her. He didn't say much of anything.

Lisa worked at her dad's pawnshop. But they had an argument, and he fired her for stealing. Lisa turned around and opened her own pawnshop, the Silver Lode, dropping out of school to run it. She bought and sold anything.

Anything.

Bikes. Watches. Hockey equipment.

Paintings. Video games. Firearms. Other things too.

Sometimes she'd tell me she needed something special. "I've got a customer who really wants a *Spectacular Spider-Man* issue 200," she'd say. "There's a comic convention this Saturday. Booth seventeen will have one. Maybe the dealer knows where you could find another?"

I would go to the show and knock something over. While attention was somewhere else, the comic would go inside my backpack or into the lining of my coat.

That was how I started as a thief.

For seven years I was the best. I made a lot of money, most of it for Lisa Wan. Then came the Peace Valley Apartments job.

A divorced woman wanted some jewelry that her ex-husband had kept. A necklace, three rings and a Cartier watch. She didn't care how she got it, so she talked to a friend, who talked to another friend, who put her in touch with Lisa. Lisa, of course, hired me.

The ex-husband lived on the top floor of the Peace Valley Apartments building downtown. He kept the jewelry in a safe. It could be opened only by his thumbprint.

Getting those jewels would be an impossible job for most people. Not for me.

How did I do it?

I don't like to give away too many of my secrets.

But okay.

I followed the husband to his country club. He gave his keys to a valet. The valet parked his car, then hung the keys on a board in her office. When the valet left to park another car, I snuck in and borrowed the keys long enough to make copies. Lisa helped me clone the electronic fob that opened the parking garage of the ex-husband's apartment.

Now I could get in whenever I wanted. The best part? I returned the keys before the valet needed them. No one was the wiser.

One night when the ex-husband was away, I used the fob to drive into the garage, then took the elevator up to the top floor. I had a key, but I could have picked the lock. Soon I was inside the apartment.

What about the safe and the thumbprint?

Sorry. That secret stays with me.

The woman was happy to get back her jewels. Lisa was happy to get paid. After she gave me my share, I was happy too. Everyone was happy all around.

Except the husband. He'd heard about Lisa and suspected she had helped his ex-wife. He told the police what he thought had happened. Now the police were looking at Lisa's shop.

A few days later Officer Phil Kushida knocked on my door. He said he had a warrant to search Kidd's Restaurant and Bar.

Phil and I had grown up together, though he'd gone to a private school. He would often come by the restaurant for eggs and coffee or sometimes just to chat. Never for work. If Phil suspected me before this, he never let on.

"Go ahead," I told him. I wasn't worried. I never kept anything at the restaurant.

Phil looked around half-heartedly, like he didn't really expect to find anything. Until he opened the till. Inside it was the necklace, lying on top of the tray of five-dollar bills.

Phil looked almost as shocked as I felt. Almost. I didn't say anything as he placed me under arrest.

The woman said I'd threatened her and forced her to tell me where her husband kept the jewels. Remember when I said robbery involves force? That made-up threat is why I was charged with robbery.

No one believed me, except for Dean. And maybe Phil. I was charged and convicted. One year in prison.

The judge told me she had to be severe to help set me straight. "You're still quite young," she said. "There's enough time left for you to get your life back on track. But you have to want it, Miss Kidd."

I don't know why or how, but I know Lisa Wan arranged my arrest. I guess she wanted the police to stop looking so closely at the Silver Lode. Lisa cost me a year of my life.

❖

I was angry when I went inside. I wanted revenge. Dean made me see things differently.

Aunt Jessie had passed on by then. Dean was the only one who visited me. He told me that business at Kidd's was picking up. If I wanted to cook or tend bar, I could do pretty well. And I wouldn't have to take any risks.

"This is a chance to start over," Dean said. "You can do anything you want."

"But I'm only good at one thing."

"Just because you're good, Ali, doesn't mean you have to do it. Your life is yours. Give it a try. Please?"

I promised I would once I got out.

Prison was a lot like detention, only scarier. I worked in the kitchen, peeling potatoes, cleaning dishes, sometimes making stew or mac and cheese.

And what I discovered about cooking was that I didn't hate it.

With a little creativity you could take ordinary ingredients and make something special. You could remind someone of home or open their taste buds to a totally new experience. There's not much variety in a prison kitchen, but I made do. I began to look forward to getting out and working with Dean.

I decided I was done as a thief. I wanted something better.

My days inside crept along, until finally my last day arrived. I was released, and I stepped outside the gate, breathing free air. It was cold outside. I looked around the parking lot for Dean. He would be driving a silver Volvo. The car had been Aunt Jessie's. It was small, and Dean looked uncomfortable crouched in the driver's seat. But my brother always gets attached to things. His glove, the restaurant, that junk pile of a car. I'll admit, I was even looking forward to seeing it.

Only that morning I didn't see the Volvo in the parking lot. There were only two cars, and they were both new. Had something happened? Maybe the car had broken down. I went back inside and asked if there were any messages. None for Alison Kidd.

I waited ten minutes. Twenty. An hour. Still no sight of Dean.

Now I was getting worried.

TWO

AS A KID Dean had what's called a developmental disability. He was slow to learn reading and math. But he was great at other things. Aunt Jessie used to say, "Smart isn't what you're born with. Smart is how you use what you're born with." It's true.

I was a good student and a top athlete, and I ended up in prison. Dean barely made it through tenth grade, but he was running one of the best restaurants in the city. He did it with hard work, but also with smart decisions.

Dean was always in a rush as a kid. Because of that his work was sloppy. Then Aunt Jessie told him to stop—not just to slow down, but to stop completely.

"Figure out what's most important. Do that first. Do it as well as you can. Then move on to the next thing."

Simple advice, but it worked for Dean. When people called him slow, they missed the point. He was accurate. He was consistent. He cared about what he did.

In the kitchen Dean got good by following recipes to the letter. If something had to cook at four hundred degrees for twenty minutes, he made sure it cooked for that time at that temperature. He paid attention. Soon he was writing his own recipes.

"The first rule," he said to me when he visited me in prison, "is always watch what you're doing."

Again, it seems simple, but how many people really watch? When I started in the prison mess, I had fifty tasks, and I rushed between them. Food got burned. Dishes were only half washed. I wasn't watching what I was doing. But I learned to.

It had been different when I was a thief. When I was on a job, no one could be more careful. I watched everything, was aware of everything. I was full of nervous excitement. The thought of failure, of being caught, forced me to focus.

Dean didn't need that fear to focus. When he said he'd do something, it got done.

So where was he now?

After waiting for another hour, I phoned a taxi and left the prison. I had a bag with some clothes and a book Dean had given me. My wallet was nearly empty. I barely had enough money to pay for the ride to Dean's place.

The front door to Kidd's was locked. The big neon sign was dark. A *SORRY—WE'RE CLOSED* sign sat in the window.

Closed? This wasn't a holiday. Maybe Dean had taken the night off to spend time with me. Even so, he had other employees who could have covered his shift. Why was the restaurant closed?

Dean still lived in the apartment above Kidd's. The door was around back, up a flight of stairs. A tall locked gate blocked the bottom of the staircase. On the gate was a sign that said *NO TRESPASSING—PRIVATE*.

When had he put up the gate? That hadn't been there before. Was he worried about someone trying to break in?

I examined the lock on the gate. With the right tools I could have picked it. But I didn't have those tools, and I didn't want them. I reminded myself I was retired from the thief business.

Retired or not, I was still worried about my brother. I set my bag down near the gate, out of the rain. I jumped and grabbed hold of the top of the gate. The metal was slippery, but I pulled myself up and swung my right leg over.

I hadn't done this in a while. I'd meant to let myself down slowly, but my shoes had no grip. I dropped down hard on the other side of the gate.

Up the staircase. I knocked on Dean's door. No answer. His blinds were shut.

Dean had always kept his spare key under the door mat. I lifted up a corner of the mat. No key.

Should I break in? I could crack a window or force the door. If Dean was in trouble, I needed to know.

I decided I wouldn't break in. Thieves break in. I wasn't a thief anymore. I'd have to find another way.

On the railing at the top of the stairs was a planter box. Dean was growing herbs. Rosemary and thyme. Maybe he'd moved the key? I lifted the box.

No key.

As I set it down my fingers felt something metallic stuck to the bottom of the box. I pried it off with my fingernail. Dean had taped his spare key to the bottom.

I unlocked the door and went inside.

Dean's home was small. The heat was off. The bed was unmade, and a pile of cooking books covered the couch. On the wall was a picture of Aunt Jessie, Dean and me. Happier times.

The bedroom and living room looked the same as always. Only the kitchen looked different. It was small but crammed full of old and new appliances. A blender, food processor, pressure cooker, slow cooker and pasta machine covered the counter. Dean still

24

had Aunt Jessie's old toaster, the kind with the sides that open like butterfly wings.

Everything was clean. Nothing looked like it had been used recently. His fridge was nearly empty, and his freezer held only a loaf of bread. Dean hadn't been here in at least a few days.

There was no desk or computer in the apartment. That didn't surprise me. Dean conducted all his business from the office at the back of the restaurant. If I wanted to learn what he'd been doing before he disappeared, I'd have to get in there.

I locked up and replaced the key. It was still raining heavily. I thought about the promise I'd made to Dean and to myself.

You don't have to be a thief if you don't want to, Ali, I told myself.

I didn't want to. But I needed to find my brother.

The front door of Kidd's had a strong double lock and a good security system.

I'd installed it myself. I could have picked the lock if I'd had the tools, but it would have taken at least fifteen minutes. Even on a rainy night, that was a long time to be standing in the street. Anyone could come along.

I climbed back over the gate at the bottom of the staircase. It was a little easier the second time. I could have opened it from the inside, I guess. But to be honest, climbing felt pretty good.

I rescued my bag, then moved along to the back entrance of Kidd's. The double doors were used for deliveries. The lock was good but nothing special. I could have opened it with a simple pick and tension tool.

Near the door were three aluminum trash cans. Empty, which was another sign the restaurant hadn't been open today. The cans were old, and the edges on the lids were ragged.

I twisted off a small piece of metal and began shaping it into a pick. Aluminum wasn't a good material—too bendy—but it would work for a single use.

That's all this is, I told myself. A single use. I just need to get into the restaurant. Just because I'm picking my way in it doesn't mean I'm going back to my old ways.

I found a small scrap of metal I could use as a tension tool. The metal was sharp. I took a pair of socks from my bag and wrapped my hands to protect them as I shaped the metal.

I heard a splash in the alley, like a foot stepping in a puddle. I didn't see anyone. I slowly counted to three hundred, listening. No other noises. I was alone. I approached the back door and told myself what I was going to do was necessary.

The second my hands touched the door, a powerful white light snapped on, aimed right at me and throwing my shadow across the door.

"Freeze right there," a voice said.

The light was directed away from my eyes. From the shadows a tall man approached. He was wearing a police uniform. My heart sank as I realized the trouble I was in.

THREE

"STEP AWAY FROM the door," the officer said. I did as I was told. But as I did, I slipped the two pieces of metal down the neck of the sock and let it drop to the ground behind me. I approached with my hands up.

The officer didn't have a weapon in his hand. Just the flashlight. Up close I could see that his face was handsome, clean-shaven and familiar.

He recognized me too. "Ali Kidd?"

"Hi, Phil. Just making your rounds?"

Phil Kushida smiled. "I thought I saw someone about to break in," he said.

"Nope. Just me. I'm looking for Dean."

"You're not the only one," Phil said. "He hasn't been in the restaurant for days. I've been asking around. No one seems to know where he is."

That wasn't like Dean. If something had happened to him—

I put the thought out of my mind.

"Now that you're out, we should talk things over," Phil said. "How about I buy you a cup of coffee?"

"I could use one," I said. "Sounds good."

"Okay, follow me."

Phil started down the alley, then stopped. He pointed at the ground near my feet.

"Looks like you dropped something," he said. A smile crossed his face. "A sock, it looks like. Don't want to lose one of those."

◆

Phil and I were friends. We'd seen a lot of each other at the restaurant, and once or twice he'd questioned me about my other line of work. He was good at his job, fair and, best of all, had never caught me.

Well, the one time. But I'd been set up, and that shouldn't count.

At an all-night coffee shop down the street from Kidd's, Phil ordered coffee for us and a grilled cheese sandwich for himself. I was too nervous to think about food. The coffee was warm. I dried my hair with some napkins.

"You just got out today?" Phil asked.

"Somehow I think you already know the answer to that," I said. "Dean was supposed to pick me up."

"I was in the restaurant three days ago. Dean wasn't there. The staff hadn't seen him. They were worried."

"So am I."

"Ali," Phil said, "did Dean talk to you about any problems he might be having? Anything financial?"

"Nothing like that, no." Dean hadn't mentioned any trouble at the restaurant or with his finances. He'd seemed a little nervous the last time he visited, but prison always made him nervous.

"Last week I stopped by Kidd's for breakfast," Phil said. "I wanted to say hi to Dean. To ask him when you were getting out."

"Checking up on me, huh?"

Phil blushed. He hid his face by biting into his sandwich. Still chewing, he said, "Dean was on the phone, talking to someone. He looked worried. I waited till he was finished and asked him what was up. 'Trouble with the bank,' he said."

"That's not possible. Dean is good with his money. He pays his taxes early, for crying out loud." My voice was getting louder, and I couldn't hide the worry I was feeling.

"It doesn't make sense to me either," Phil said. "Unless maybe he was lying."

"Maybe he doesn't trust you," I said.

"Why wouldn't he? We're friends."

That was true. Dean had always liked Phil. When some neighborhood kids had broken windows and spray-painted the restaurant, Phil had found them and warned them not to do it again. Since then Kidd's had been graffiti-free.

"There's no reason for Dean not to trust me," Phil said.

"You did put me in jail," I said.

Phil scowled. "I didn't know I was going to find anything when I searched the restaurant."

"Neither did I."

Phil put his sandwich down and looked at me seriously. "If you ever want to do something

33

about the person who set you up—if you ever want to tell me your side of the story—"

"I appreciate it, Phil, but there's nothing to tell."

"So Lisa Wan goes free," he said.

"I don't want anything more to do with Lisa Wan. I'm done with her. Retired."

"Very glad to hear that," Phil said. "I'll keep asking around about your brother. If you don't hear from him in twenty-four hours, let me know and I'll file a report. In the meantime, Ali, do you have somewhere to stay?"

"Dean left me a key to his apartment," I said. It wasn't a total lie.

"Good. Stay there, and I'll call if I learn anything. Promise?"

I didn't respond right away.

"Ali," Phil said, "the worst thing you can do right now is get yourself jammed up all over again. You just got out today. You don't want to go back, do you?"

"I'm never going back," I said.

"I really hope that's true, Ali." Phil smiled. He patted my hand. "I promise you I'll do everything I can to find Dean."

"Thanks," I said. But his comments only made me worry more. If the police couldn't find Dean, then where could my brother be?

Phil insisted on walking me back to Kidd's. Thankfully, he didn't stick around to make sure I got inside. I didn't want to have to explain why I was climbing over the gate.

Inside Dean's apartment, I put two pieces of frozen bread into the toaster and searched through the kitchen and living room. There were a few bank statements in the trash, along with some junk mail. Nothing suspicious. It looked like the restaurant was making a profit, and Dean was paying his bills on time.

I had toast and jam and continued looking around. Dean had wrapped the toaster's cord with electrical tape. Aunt Jessie would have been happy that the machine was still getting used. She liked to repair things rather than throw them out. Dean was like that too.

There was nothing hidden beneath Dean's bed. I looked through his clothing. Nothing told me where he'd disappeared to or why. The problem was simple, I thought. I was looking in the wrong place.

The apartment might have been Dean's home, but he spent most of his life in the restaurant below. That was where I should be looking. I still had the makeshift lockpicks rolled up in my sock.

I'd promised Phil I'd leave it alone. But what Phil didn't know wouldn't bother him. And besides, Kidd's was Dean's real home. I was in the same building already. All I was doing was going downstairs.

Picking a lock is like painting a picture from memory. Instead of a brush you have a pick and a tension tool, sometimes called a wrench. Instead of using your eyes, you rely on feel. The pick goes inside the chamber and lifts up these little things called pins. They're often on springs, so once you raise one with the pick, you have to keep it up while you work on the others. There are all sorts of tricks and surprises to a good lock. When you've got all the pins up, you turn the wrench, which turns the chamber and opens the lock.

I guess that sounds nothing like painting, does it?

What I mean is that both are about trusting your instincts. To do that you have to practice. How do you paint a face? Or a landscape? By painting each part a thousand times. Whether it's eyes and a nose or trees and clouds, you practice each little part, from every possible direction. That way when you have to paint an entire picture, your brain treats it as a bunch of little problems to solve rather than one big impossible problem.

I can't paint at all. My faces look like scrambled eggs on a plate, and my landscapes look like a child drew them. Hands and cows defeat me every time. But before I went to prison, I could open a lock, any lock, even a tough one and even with bad tools like these.

It's a gift. I'm good at it, and I practice.

It took fifteen minutes, and I nearly broke the pick, but the lock on the back door finally, finally yielded. I walked into Kidd's for the first time in a year.

The kitchen and storeroom were neat. Dean insisted on a good cleaning before anyone went home. Nothing looked out of place. In the restaurant the chairs were piled on top of tables. The till was empty. Opening it brought back memories.

When Phil Kushida had opened the till on the day he found the necklace, I'd confessed to him right away. I had to. If I didn't, Dean might have taken some of the blame. Lisa Wan had counted on that. She'd known I would protect my brother by confessing. What had happened to me wasn't fair, but I'd deserved it more than my brother did.

Dean had never done anything to anyone. All he cared about was Kidd's. And me, I suppose. He wouldn't leave me, and he definitely wouldn't leave the restaurant, without saying something.

His office door was locked. I had it open in seven minutes. The skills were coming back. I didn't know how to feel about that—happy, worried or both.

Inside the office I saw papers piled high on Dean's desk. The small room wasn't messy, but it was too full to be comfortable. His old computer was turned off. A stack of new menus covered the chair.

In the center of his desk was his cell phone. Dean used it for deliveries, for working out payroll. He'd never leave it behind.

Not unless someone forced him to.

FOUR

THE LOCK SCREEN on my brother's cell phone asked for a four-digit code. I tried his birthday, forward and back. Both times the screen flashed red. One attempt remaining, it told me.

People usually reach into their own lives for codes, so a birthday or some other important occasion is a good place to start. Parents often use something connected to their children. Pet owners will use the names of a dog or cat.

Dean had no children or pets. He wasn't married. All he had was his work.

I sat down at his desk and looked around. Dean was probably in the restaurant when he set his passcode. That meant everything I needed to figure it out was probably here.

Four numbers. Maybe the date he opened Kidd's? No, because he'd taken it over from Aunt Jessie. Before that he'd worked in the kitchen. Dean didn't have as sharp a memory of our parents as I did. He didn't remember much of our life before coming to live with our aunt. For him, it was like he'd always been here.

So not the day he started or the day he took it over. Not a phone number—too many digits. A page in a favorite recipe book? A temperature or cooking time? I was getting desperate.

I looked at the menus. The cover image was a black-and-white drawing of the restaurant's front window. Below that were the telephone number, the address and which credit cards they accepted (all major ones).

The address—778 East Fifth Street.

I punched in 7785. The screen lit up and flashed to the home screen. I was in.

The past few weeks of Dean's life were in his phone. Shift schedules for work, to-do lists, recipes he wanted to try, along with short notes on their results. Needs more punch— maybe leeks instead of green onions?

He'd received three calls from a company called Ajax Credit. I searched the name and found they specialized in debts and finance. Flexible rates and options, said the website.

I opened Dean's banking app, using the same numbers. Dean had a line of credit with a $10,000 limit. The amount owed was currently at $400, with a payment scheduled for the end of the month. My brother owed nothing.

I phoned Ajax Credit. After five rings a smooth male voice said, "How may I help you?"

"I'm phoning on behalf of Dean Kidd," I said. "I'm wondering why you called him last week."

"What is your relationship to Mr. Kidd?" the voice asked.

"Sister. I work with him too. I mean, I will be."

"Apologies, ma'am," the smooth voice said. "We don't give out the information of our clients without their approval."

"So Dean is a client?" I said.

The voice seemed slightly flustered. "I can't help you, ma'am. Don't call back. Goodbye."

Of course I called right back.

"Ma'am—" he began.

"My brother is missing," I said. "If he is in trouble, if he owes someone money, I need to know. Please help me."

"We have a policy, ma'am."

"Well, good for you." I hung up on him.

After checking the rest of the information stored on the phone, I turned it off. I looked around the office. Even with all the junk, the place seemed empty. Like a car missing its engine or a body without a heart, Kidd's was nothing without Dean.

There was something off about Ajax Credit, something strange about the voice on the phone. Their address for Ajax was in the financial district, on the second floor above a currency exchange. The office would be closed by the time I got there.

I decided that might be a good thing.

＞ ◆ ＜

The taxi dropped me on the corner near the Ajax office. I paid with some cash I'd found in Dean's office. Technically this was stealing, but Dean would understand.

The currency exchange was in an old

gray concrete building three stories tall. Through the large glass windows I could see black bulbs on the inside walls. Security cameras.

Ajax Credit had a small sign in a window on the second floor. The blinds were shut, and the lights were off.

I walked past the building without looking in the window, keeping my face partly turned away.

On the corner I looked up. A light was on in a room on the third floor, directly above Ajax. The blinds were half-open. I could see the back of a head, a pair of shoulders. Another figure moving around the room.

I stepped backward into the street to get a better view. The shoulders were large and broad, and the head was egg-shaped with a fringe of dark brown hair. The person was facing away from the window.

But it was Dean. I could tell.

I couldn't see who the second person was. I saw movement near the edge of the window.

A loud horn blasted, a sound like *flonnn*! I turned my head and saw a car heading straight toward me. I jumped up onto the curb as it passed, spraying water at my legs.

Dean was in that room. He hadn't moved. Maybe he was tied up. I couldn't see his face, but I knew it was him. He needed help.

On the side of the building was a short staircase. I climbed it and tried the door. Locked. Through the glass in the door I could see an elevator at the end of a short hallway. Above the elevator was another black security-camera bubble. I could maybe pick the lock, but I'd be caught on camera while doing it.

I backed away from the door. There didn't seem to be another entrance. Maybe in the alley?

But the alley was a no-go. Two old men gathered bottles from a nearby dumpster. The building's exit door had no handles or keyhole. It opened only from inside.

There weren't any good options. I thought of phoning Phil Kushida. He wouldn't be happy to know I'd done the opposite of what I'd promised him. I would call him if I couldn't rescue Dean myself.

Maybe Dean was up there willingly, I thought.

On the other hand, maybe the person keeping him there had a gun or knife. I wasn't a fighter. I was a thief.

No, not anymore, I reminded myself.

I wasn't going to steal. I wasn't even going to break in. All I was going to do was get a little exercise.

I waited until there were no cars coming down the street, then walked up the stairs and stood to the left of the door, where the camera couldn't see me. A scrolled concrete arch hung above the doorway. By standing on that, I could probably reach the ledge of the third-floor window.

If I couldn't? It would be quite a fall.

My shoes were cheap and had no tread. I took them off, along with my socks. The concrete was cold and wet.

I jumped and caught hold of the lip of the arch. I put the ball of my foot against the building and slowly, carefully, climbed up. I rested on the top of the arch for a second, looking down. The drop was fifteen feet. I'd been up much higher before, but not in a while.

Headlights shone at the end of the street. A taxi turned and cruised by. I lay flat against the wall and hoped the driver wouldn't look my way.

The lights grew small and disappeared.

I stood and felt along the wall. The building's surface was rough, but there were no handholds. Nothing to step on. The window ledge was seven feet above me and two feet to my left. I'd have to jump.

There wasn't much room for a running start. I got ready. Took two quick steps and sprang, stretching my arms out, watching as my left hand slapped the ledge and gripped onto it.

My right hand missed.

For a second I was falling, and then my left hand took my body's weight. My arm began to burn. I flung my right arm onto the ledge, my feet trying to run up the wall. I pulled myself up until I could throw one leg onto the ledge, then the other.

The ledge was narrow. Looking down made me dizzy. It had been a while since I'd done any serious climbing. Usually I had rope. And proper footwear.

Looking through the window, I saw Dean seated in a wooden chair. His arms were tied behind his back with wire. Something was wrapped around his head. He was struggling.

I dug my fingers into the edge of the window and pulled. The glass slid open a little. It wasn't locked, but it probably hadn't been opened in a long while.

When I'd worked the window open enough to squeeze through, I crouched and swung my body feetfirst into the room. Hearing noise behind him, Dean tried to turn around. He was shaking his head, rocking the chair beneath him.

It was an office suite, empty except for the chair. The carpet was gray and soft. I untwisted the wire around Dean's wrists. A handkerchief had been taped over his mouth. As soon as I ripped it off, he said, "You shouldn't be here, Ali. You gotta get out right now."

"Some thanks," I said. "I'm here to rescue you, Dean. But if you'd rather stay tied to the chair for the rest of your life—"

"You don't understand," Dean said. "They planned it. They wanted you to find me."

"What does that mean?"

Before he could answer, I heard clapping, loud and slow. The door opened. A man in a gray suit entered, holding a gun. Behind him was Lisa Wan.

"You've still got the skills, Ali," Lisa said.

FiVE

LISA LOOKED THE same as ever. Her clothes were black and well-tailored. Her hair was cut short. Platinum bracelets adorned her arms, and a platinum chain hung around her neck. Her smile looked like a wolf's. With Lisa Wan, there was no question who was in charge.

"You deserve a better party for getting out of jail," she said. "But there will be plenty of time to celebrate once we're done."

She turned to the man with the gun. "Ali and Dean are old friends of mine, Max. You don't need to point the gun at them. Unless they try to leave."

The man in the gray suit nodded. He tucked the gun inside his suit jacket.

"What happened to Monster?" I asked.

"An unlucky accident," Lisa said. "He'll be away for four more years. Max is doing just as well. That was him you talked to on the phone."

Max smiled at me. His hair was gray, and his eyes light blue. He looked much older than Lisa. I wondered how he'd come to work for her.

There were red marks on Dean's wrists, but he seemed to be all right. "I need to get my brother home," I told Lisa.

"Soon enough. Let's talk for a while. You can sit down, if you like."

"I'm not talking with you," I said. "We

have nothing to say to each other."

"We have so much," she said. "Like your brother's debts. Let's talk about those to start."

"Dean doesn't have any debts. His credit line is at zero." I turned to Dean. "Right?"

Dean looked down at the floor.

"He owes me $17,000," Lisa said. "To be more accurate, he owes Ajax Credit $17,000. Can you pay that debt for him?"

"How is that even possible?" I asked.

"It's my fault," Dean said. "I had some bad luck, and I made some bad decisions."

"Your brother is quite the gambler," Lisa said.

Dean still wouldn't look me in the eye. "I don't know how it all happened," he said. "I got a tip to bet on this race. I was winning, and I thought I could buy a new stove and fridge for the restaurant. Then I started to lose. I don't remember much after that, but when I woke up, I saw the paper I'd signed."

Lisa pulled a paper from her pocket and unfolded it. "A promissory note," she said. "Dean Kidd agrees to pay the sum of $17,000 to Ajax Credit."

"It's a scam," I said. "A trick."

"No," Lisa said, "it's a legal document."

Dean had never gambled, as far as I knew. Someone working for Lisa must have tricked him. I'd seen it before. A man offers you a tip on a horse race. A sure thing, he says. You bet a few dollars, something small. Surprise, surprise, you win. Your five dollars is now a hundred. When the man comes back, you trust him enough to bet large.

That is how they get you.

Still, Dean would never have bet as much as $17,000. As far as I knew, he'd never even seen that much money. Lisa was an expert at making people do things they wouldn't normally do. Somehow she'd convinced Dean to bet money he didn't have, and to think that it was his own fault.

Lisa folded the paper and put it back in her pocket. "It doesn't matter how it happened," she said. She always seemed to know what I was thinking. "All that matters is your brother owes us."

"They're going to take the restaurant," Dean said. Tears were forming in his eyes. Kidd's wasn't just his business or the place he'd grown up. It was his childhood, it was Aunt Jessie, it was where he felt comfortable.

"No crying now, Dean," Lisa said. "We don't want to take Kidd's from you. We don't want to see you or your sister out in the street. Nobody wants that, do they?" She looked at me.

"What do you want?" I said.

"Nothing unreasonable, Ali. I just want you to come back to work."

As much as I hated her at that moment, I had to admit that Lisa Wan was a genius. A sick genius, but a genius nonetheless.

She knew I would never work for her again without a compelling reason. The only way was if Dean was in trouble. Ajax Credit was an even better front for her criminal business than the pawnshop.

Dean and I could try to fight it. Refuse to pay and take Ajax Credit to court. But Dean had signed the paper, and the court wouldn't care how he'd built up a gambling debt of that size. We might lose the case. Or we might win, but the lawyer fees would cost us more than the debt.

I thought of calling Phil Kushida, confessing everything. He'd been after Lisa Wan for years. I trusted Phil. But I couldn't trust him to outsmart Lisa or to make sure

Dean wasn't harmed in the process.

Lisa had planted evidence to put me in jail. Now she was telling me she wanted my help. In both cases I had no choice. I had to look out for my brother. If there was another solution, I couldn't see it.

Or maybe I didn't want to.

"What's the job?" I asked.

"A piece of art. A photograph."

"That doesn't sound so hard."

Lisa smiled. "It's impossible, Ali. Why else would I come to you?"

◆

A few days after I'd started my sentence in prison, Lisa told me, an elderly woman came into Lisa's pawnshop with a box of old photographs and postcards. Lisa paid the woman five dollars for the whole box. She put the box of photos in a corner, wrote *$1 each/3 for $5* on the front of the box and went back to her desk.

Six weeks later a man came in. He was blond and handsome, though his nose had been broken before, and he was missing some teeth. He looked around the store and started sifting through the box of photos.

Lisa was thinking about other things. She didn't worry too much about the man. The next person to enter was a beautiful woman, who walked over to see what the man was doing.

"Find anything, Ty?" she asked.

"Maybe." The man was trying not to sound excited, but Lisa could tell he was fascinated by the box. He was too careful with the photos, treating each one like it was precious.

"Ty, I want to go," the woman said. "I'm hungry."

The man took his time walking to the counter. "Three for five, huh?" he said to Lisa.

"That was the old price," Lisa said. She didn't know what the box was worth, but the man was too interested in the photos for them to be junk. She decided to overcharge him, then look up what the photos were worth much later. "New price is $500. All or nothing. Take it or leave it."

She knew she'd made a mistake when the man smiled.

"Deal," he said, slapping five $100 bills on the counter. He walked out, happy, with the box under his arm.

"What's so special about a bunch of old pictures?" Lisa heard the woman ask him. The two were holding hands as they left.

"These are Jane Brick photos," the man said. "Originals. They're beautiful—and worth a lot of money."

⟩ ◆ ⟨

I didn't know anything about photography—or painting or anything else—but I'd heard of Jane Brick. She'd done wonderful photos of city streets in the 1960s and '70s. Now her photos fetched high prices, were featured in museums and private collections, and were sold as posters and greeting cards. She'd had a very sad life and passed away young.

Lisa explained that Jane's mother had talked about a "missing" collection of Jane's photos. Ten shots taken around her home. When Jane's mother passed, a distant cousin cleaned out their house. She was the one who had sold the box to Lisa. She hadn't known or cared what they were.

Lisa had made $495 on the box without doing anything. But she talked about it like the man had stolen millions from her.

The man who'd bought the box was named Ty Collins. He was thirty-four years old and retired. A former hockey player, he'd won the Hart Memorial Trophy and made the playoffs twice. Now he collected art. Photographs mostly.

COLLINS SCORES IN OVERTIME WITH PHOTO FIND read the headline in the local paper. Collins had paid to have an expert look at the photos to verify that they were taken by Jane Brick. The reporter mentioned Collins's "remarkable eye" for spotting the similarities between the pictures and Brick's other work.

Collins was having each photo framed. They would be displayed in his penthouse suite for one year, then donated to the city's art gallery. "I'm just happy to bring these photos to the world," he was quoted as saying.

Lisa Wan was furious.

"That dumb ape got lucky and cheated me," she said.

"Let me get all this straight, so I understand," I said. "He bought these from you for a hundred times what you paid, and now you want me to steal them back?"

"That's only part of it," Lisa said. "I want the photos, yes. But I want him to be embarrassed. He needs to know he's not smarter than me."

"So you don't want me to steal the photos?"

"You're not just going to steal them," Lisa said. "You're going to replace them."

SİX

WHAT LISA WANTED wasn't impossible. Not for me anyway. But it was closer to impossible than I'd ever been before.

"You're going to take his photos," Lisa said. "We'll copy them and replace them with fakes. When it's discovered, he'll look like an idiot for buying them. Then the originals will magically show up in my shop."

"All of that work just to fool someone who paid you a lot of money fair and square?"

"He's a lucky fool," Lisa said.

Max had left the room. When he returned he was holding my socks and shoes. They were wet from the rain. I put them on anyway.

"You haven't lost your skills," Lisa said. "You managed to find us and get to your brother with no problem. All you have to do to rescue him is complete this job."

"And you'll erase his debt?"

"Completely. I promise."

A promise from Lisa Wan wasn't worth the time it took to hear it. But there were no choices open to me.

Dean sighed. "I'm sorry, Ali," he said.

Lisa ran a hand through his hair. The emerald ring on her finger gleamed. "Don't be sorry, Dean. Your sister was meant to do this. And you want to know a secret? Secretly she wants to."

I pulled her hand off my brother's head. "Don't talk to him or touch him," I said.

"From here on out, you leave my brother alone."

Lisa's face flashed anger. She calmed herself and sighed. "All right."

"I will look at the job," I said. "If I think it can't be done, I'm walking away."

"You would do that? The Great Ali Kidd admitting defeat?"

"I'm retired," I said. "These are special circumstances."

Lisa smiled. "Whatever you say."

> ◆ <

Before she let us go, Lisa gave me $300 for expenses. Not only was I breaking all my promises, but I was even taking money from the person who had sent me to jail.

In the taxi ride home, Dean said, "You don't have to do this, Ali. We can tell Phil what happened. Maybe he can help."

"It's our word against Lisa's," I said. "She has your signature on the note saying you owe her money. Even if Phil could prove she did something wrong, he couldn't protect us. Lisa would set fire to the restaurant or hurt us or something. She's smart. She's covered all the angles."

"Do you really think you can pull off that job without being caught?"

I didn't answer right away. There were a number of factors that would make it difficult. I listed them in my head.

1. Ty Collins was rich. He'd have the best security system money could buy. That was no problem really. I'd handled high-tech security before.

2. Collins was not only rich but also famous. People paid attention to him. His home would be designed to keep strange people away.

3. I wasn't a professional forger. Photos

were probably much easier to forge than paintings. But it would still be a difficult process. If Collins could tell that the pictures were taken by Jane Brick, he might be able to tell an original from a copy.

4. I wouldn't just have to break in. I'd have to break in twice. Once to take the photos to copy them, then again to sneak back in and replace them. Either that or carry the copying equipment in with me.

5. Now that I had a criminal record, the police and security would pay extra attention to me. I would get no breaks. Not even from Phil Kushida. As much as I liked Phil, as much as he was my friend, I was going to have to stay away from him until this was over.

There they were. Five good reasons not to do the job. Yet all of them were less important than reason number six.

Lisa.

She had already betrayed me once. There was no guarantee she wouldn't do it again if she got the chance. If I did this job for her, I'd be placing myself in a position where I'd have to trust her.

Inviting the wolf back in for a second time. What big feet you have, Grandma.

"I really don't know," I told my brother. "It will be tough. If I can't pull it off, I'll have to think of something else."

As the taxi pulled onto our street, I saw movement. A truck was parked across the street from Kidd's. Someone was sitting in the front seat, watching the restaurant.

It was a bad sign. Another one. We went inside quickly and locked the door behind us.

＞ ◆ ＜

In the morning I walked to the library, bought myself a coffee from the vending machine and began doing research on Ty Collins.

He lived in the West End, in a penthouse suite with a view of the harbor. He'd played in the NHL for eleven years, from age nineteen to thirty, on six different teams. He was engaged to a model named Becky Sylvester. They donated money to several local charities and were featured in the Society section of the newspaper almost every week.

Collins's mother had been a photographer. He'd become interested because of her. "Paintings are rare," he said in an interview. "There's only one original. But with a photograph, everyone can have the same one." That was why he would be donating the Jane Brick pictures the following year.

I looked at Collins's website. His next personal appearance was at a charity dinner in two weeks. He was receiving an award for his donations. Ty Collins seemed liked a decent guy. Robbing him wouldn't be much fun.

There was a number on the website for his publicity agent. I phoned it from the hallway of the library. A voice that sounded stuffed up said, "Who may I ask is calling?"

"My name is Lisa Ajax," I said, speaking the first two words that came to mind. "I write for a photography magazine in New York. I'm in town briefly, and I'd like to talk to Mr. Collins about his discovery."

"Which magazine is that?" the agent asked.

"It's just called Photography."

"Of course," he said. I didn't know if he was pretending to know it or if the magazine actually existed. "Would one o'clock today work?"

"Uh, sure," I said.

"He'll show you the photos. No questions about hockey, okay? Only the pictures."

"That's all I care about," I said.

"Good. Here's the address."

I had just enough time to get back to Dean's apartment. I dressed in an old checked shirt of his, tied my hair back and put on a pair of old red-framed glasses. They'd belonged to Aunt Jessie. Dean kept them on the mantel.

"Can you even see through those?" Dean asked.

The lenses were grimy, and they distorted things. Dean looked nine feet wide. I pushed them down my nose and looked over the top of them.

"Do you have a voice recorder?" I asked.

"Only on my phone."

"Then how about a pad and pen?"

My brother had a box of pads, the kind the wait staff used to take down orders. He found me an old pencil in a kitchen drawer.

Ten minutes later I was on my way to Collins's apartment.

SEVEN

THE BUILDING IN which Collins lived was thirty stories tall. The outside was smooth mirrored glass. Nothing to hold on to and no way to climb.

At the front door I buzzed apartment 3001. A voice on the intercom said, "Hello?"

Above the speaker was a small monitor and camera. Collins could see me, and I could see him.

"I'm here to look at the photos," I said.

"Miss Ajax, right? I'll let you in. Take the elevator on the left."

I heard a buzz and click as the door unlocked. Inside was a long, bright foyer with a high ceiling and a marble floor. Paintings of horses and castles hung on the walls.

The leftmost elevator was open and waiting. I stepped inside. The buttons only went up to floor twenty-five. To get to the top floors, you needed a key or someone to buzz you up. Another camera stared at me from above the panel. The doors closed once I was inside, and the elevator started moving. We were on floor thirty in less than fifteen seconds.

As I stepped out of the elevator, I looked for a staircase or fire escape. To the right was a door marked EMERGENCY EXIT. It was locked.

So Ty Collins's building was unclimbable. To get to his apartment he'd have to see me at the door and in the elevator. He had total control over who came to his floor.

I didn't have to knock on Collins's door. A tall Asian woman with a blond streak in her hair opened it. This must be Becky Sylvester. She smiled and said, "Ty is in the study."

I'd never been in a home with a study before. (Well, that wasn't really true. I mean I'd never been invited into one.) The ceilings were high, and the furniture was dark, rich wood. The entire far wall was glass, looking out over beach and water.

The study had one shelf of books, another of trophies. A TV was mounted over the fireplace. Ty Collins was sitting in a brown leather chair. A silver tea set sat on a glass table.

Becky sat down in a chair next to Ty. "We were just having tea," she said. "Want some?"

I accepted a cup. As Becky poured, I asked Ty Collins about the photos.

"They're amazing," he said. "My mom was a great fan of Jane Brick."

"How did you know the photos were real?"

"It was a bit of a gamble," he said. "I was 90 percent sure. When the pawnshop lady raised the price, I became 99 percent sure. But I liked the pictures a lot. If they hadn't turned out to be Jane Brick originals, I'd still be happy to display them."

"They must be very valuable," I said.

"Of course."

"Has anyone offered to buy them?"

"A company wanted to pay me $300,000 for the set," he said. "Another company offered $150,000 for one of them."

"But you won't sell?"

"They don't belong to me," Collins said. "They belong to everybody. I was just lucky to find them."

"You have a beautiful home, Mr. Collins."

"We like it very much, thank you."

"Tell us about yourself," Becky said. "How long have you been a journalist?"

I had thought about the life of Lisa Ajax on the ride over. The question wasn't a surprise. "Seven years," I said. "I started in college. I've only been working for the magazine for a little while."

We made small talk for a few minutes, until Becky stood up. "I have to go pick up my dress for tomorrow," she said. "Nice meeting you, Ms. Ajax."

"You too," I said.

Once she had left I asked Ty, "What's happening tomorrow?"

"Oh, just a little ceremony. Becky and I are getting an award for fundraising."

"Congratulations."

"Thanks. It's a little embarrassing. Getting an award for giving." He seemed uncomfortable. "Let's look at those photos, shall we?"

He led me across the apartment to a small room with a locked door. Attached to the handle was a keypad.

"Would you please look away for a sec?" he said.

I stared at the glass wall, trying to catch a reflection. Collins was careful. He cupped his left hand around the keypad as his right hand punched in the code.

The lock hissed and spun. The door opened.

The room was smaller than the study but still larger than Dean's whole apartment. It had no windows. The walls were painted white. There were two comfortable chairs inside. No other furniture.

The Jane Brick photos took up one wall. They showed a street corner, small houses and 1960s cars, with snowy mountains in the background. The light was different in each picture. Some glowed a bright summer yellow.

Others a stormy gray. Still others were a warm peach color or a soft rose.

"Jane would photograph the same place at different times," Ty said. "She could make an ordinary street look like paradise. Or the opposite. Or anything in between."

"They're amazing," I said. And I meant it. The photos were beautiful. Even the creases and fade marks added to their beauty.

Ty explained how he'd had the photos matted and framed to make sure they were protected from direct sunlight, acid, water and human hands. He had spent several thousand dollars to protect them. "The art gallery will make sure they're preserved," he said. "They'll scan the photos and make copies and digitally restore them. But for now these are one of a kind."

"You really don't want to just keep them all to yourself?" I asked. "Even one?"

He shook his head. "I grew up poor. My mother and I could only go to the art gallery on Tuesdays, when admission was half price. There are a lot of great artists whose work we never got to see. I want to make sure folks like my mom can enjoy these photos too."

"That's very generous."

"Maybe," he said. "Or maybe I just don't want the responsibility. They're nice to have, but I don't want to spend the rest of my life being worried."

"About what?"

"About whether or not the photos will be stolen."

Collins smiled.

"They're safe for now," he said. "But I'd rather let somebody else worry about them."

EIGHT

BACK AT KIDD'S I sat in Dean's office and thought about how best to pull off the job. Ty Collins and Becky Sylvester would be out of the apartment the next night. That was as good a time as any.

I wrote out a list of the tools I'd need.

1 janitor's uniform

1 pair of work gloves

1 dust mask

1 black felt-tip marker

1 white felt-tip marker
2 panes of glass, 24 inches by 24 inches
glass cutters
hair dye, silver
photo paper from the 1960s
portable printer and scanner

The last two items were Lisa Wan's concern. My business was getting in and out with the photos and not getting caught.

Speed would be important. How quickly could I get the photos out of their frames, scan them, replace them and put the frames together again? If each photo took six minutes, that was a total of one hour. Far too long to stay in the apartment. But if I took them out of the building, scanned them somewhere else and then returned the copies, I'd have to break in twice. That was once too many. There was no easy solution. I would have to take the scanner with me and hope I was fast enough.

Dean was busy getting the restaurant

ready to open for dinner. I could tell he was nervous, making sure everything would be perfect. But he was also happy. He was doing what he was born to do, what he loved to do.

In a way that was how I felt. Planning a job like this, figuring out the details, was what I enjoyed most. It was a gift.

I told myself that was wrong. I didn't have to be something I didn't want to be. It was my choice.

Or was it?

I had to fix things with Lisa so she'd leave Dean and me alone. That meant one last job. Just because I enjoyed it a little didn't mean I wasn't going to quit. I was done after this. For good.

◆

I bought the hair dye at a pharmacy, and the rest of the materials from a hardware store.

The glass was heavy, but I carried it home on the bus.

The restaurant was busy. I stayed in the office, working on my plan. I could hear people yelling and dishes breaking on the floor. It sounded like Dean was having a tough night.

I cleaned off Dean's desk and carefully laid the glass on top.

The uniform was light brown. On the back, in black letters with a white outline, I wrote:

JOHN'S GLASS
REPAIR & INSTALLATION
CLEARLY THE BEST AROUND!

I washed the uniform in the bathroom sink, then hung it up to dry. It had to look like it had been worn a few times. While it dried, I dyed my hair.

I don't like disguises. They feel unnatural to me. Less is more, as far as I'm concerned. But Ty Collins had seen my face, and I needed to look as different as I could. Most people don't look too carefully, especially at blue-collar workers.

When I looked in the mirror, my hair was a shiny silver. I looked older, but somehow happier. More at peace. I imagined my older self, my hair turned silver naturally. Still working in the restaurant, safe and in no danger of going back to prison. It was a good future.

When I came out of the washroom, Lisa Wan was waiting in the office.

"I like the hair," she said. "It's a nice touch. Looks like you're all set."

"What do you want, Lisa?"

"It's not what I want. It's what you need."

Lisa had a nylon case with her. She put it on the desk, on top of the glass, and opened it. Inside was a small dark gray box, smaller than a laptop. It had a narrow tray on top and a long slit on its side.

"It's already loaded with the right kind of paper," Lisa said. "All you have to do is plug it in, load the photos into the tray and take the copies once they print."

"How long does it take?"

"Not long. Maybe two minutes per photo."

"And the quality is good enough?"

"It's the very best," Lisa said. "It'll fool anyone who doesn't have a microscope."

"Good," I said, sitting behind the desk.

"Speaking of fools, Ali, you better not try anything foolish with me."

"Why would I?" I asked.

"I expect you to deliver these photos to me. All ten of them. No tricks."

"That's the plan, isn't it?"

Lisa smiled. "I'm making a small change to the plan. Max will be having dinner here tomorrow night. When I get the photos, I'll tell him to leave. If I don't get them, do you know what will happen?"

"I can guess," I said. "He won't leave a tip?"

Lisa leaned over the desk so that our faces were close together. Her hands rested on the glass. Her eyes burned.

"If you want your brother to stay healthy, you'll finish this job. No mistakes. No accidents. It has to go off perfectly."

I stared back at her. "It will."

"After you have the photos, bring them to me at the pawnshop. When I get them, I'll phone Max. For your brother's sake, you better deliver."

She left without saying anything else. I stared at the door as it closed. Once she was gone, I got back to work.

NiNE

TY COLLINS AND Becky Sylvester would probably take a limousine to their charity event. I phoned the top limo company in the city, pretending to be Becky double-checking her reservation. "You tell me the time so I know you remembered my instructions," I said.

"Six forty on the dot, out front," the limo dispatcher said. "We'll be there, ma'am. Guaranteed."

That night, at 6:35, the spot in front of

the building was blocked by a black work van. The van's side door was open. The limo driver parked one space down.

Ty and Becky walked out of their apartment building at 6:51. Ty was dressed in a white tuxedo with a white shirt and tie. Becky wore a long gold dress that shimmered as she walked. A long fur coat hung over her arm.

As they approached the limo, an old woman closed the door of the van. She carried a black nylon case and held a small pane of glass by its edge. Her hair was silver. As she turned around, she didn't see Becky and stumbled right into her.

"So sorry," the old woman said. She had a slight accent, maybe Russian or Polish. She bent and picked up Becky's coat and purse. "My fault, miss. You are not too badly hurt?"

"It's all right," Becky said. "I'm okay." More important, her dress was okay. She got in the limo and didn't think twice about what had happened. Not until they got to the awards ceremony.

"I want a picture of us on the red carpet, Ty." She asked the driver, "Would you take one for us?"

"Yes, ma'am."

Becky opened her purse. Her phone wasn't there.

"Must've dropped it," she said.

"Dropped what?"

"My phone. My keys too."

"You probably left them in the apartment," Ty said.

"I'd never leave my phone."

"Well, that's true," Ty said. "Guess maybe we should go back and look."

"I'll go. Give me your keys. You go get us our table."

Ty stepped out of the limousine. Flashbulbs went off. Becky waved at the cameras before she shut the door.

At 7:03 the limo returned to the apartment building. Becky looked in the street and in the gutter. No phone and no keys. The work van was still parked out front.

Becky approached the door of the apartment. She had Ty's keys, but she didn't need them. The old woman was standing in the lobby near the elevators. She opened the door for Becky.

"Thanks," Becky said.

The old woman looked a little familiar. Her hair was silver and cut short. A dust mask covered her mouth.

"Did you happen to see my phone?" Becky asked her.

"Sorry?"

"My phone. I lost my—never mind."

The elevator doors opened. They both stepped inside. Becky punched in the code for the thirtieth floor.

As the doors began to close, she noticed

something. Her hand moved out to keep the doors open. On the table by the mailboxes sat her phone and her set of keys.

"I should hold?" the old woman asked. Her foot blocked the doors from closing.

Becky grinned in relief. She waved her hand. "No, I found what I needed. Thanks."

She returned to the limo. It was 7:07. She would still be on time. Everything would work out perfectly.

❖

I stepped out of the elevator and unlocked the door to Collins's apartment. The next time Becky Sylvester tried to use her door key, she would find it didn't work. Hopefully that would be long after I was gone.

The passcode for the elevator was 1212. Not very creative. I hoped the same code would work for the door of the photo room.

Inside the apartment, the hall light came on before I could touch the switch. Motion-activated, I guessed. The rest of the rooms were dark. The place smelled of perfume and was still humid from the shower.

I crossed to the photo room. The numbers on the keypad glowed. I entered 1212 and waited.

Nothing.

It was different from the elevator code. Okay, I could figure it out. I tried the obvious— 2121. Nothing. Then 0001. Nothing. Then 1234. Then my old friend 0000.

Nothing.

Frustrated, I put down the case. The code might be written in Ty Collins's files. Often installers will do that, even though they're not supposed to. Sometimes customers will write it down on the service contract or the warranty.

I hadn't seen a file cabinet during my interview with Ty. I looked in the bedroom, the study and another room that might have been an office but where every surface was covered with clothes. A heavy aroma of Chanel No. 5 hung in the air. Becky had used this room to get ready.

Underneath a bathrobe there was a file cabinet. It was locked. In a few seconds it wasn't. I put the bent safety pin back in my pocket and looked through the files.

Tax documents. Contracts. Warranties and service plans for dishwashers and cars. Nothing on the security system.

I looked in the study. Ty's trophies caught my eye. Maybe the four-digit code was his first year of playing professional hockey? Or the year he won his first MVP trophy? I went back to the door and tried them both, forward and reversed. Nothing.

I could break down the door. Or take it off its hinges. Or break the faceplate and try to work open the lock's mechanism. All of these choices would leave evidence that I had been here.

There was one more thing to try. I walked into the bedroom and scanned the walls. A mirror was hanging over the dresser. I moved it, uncovering a fuse box. I opened it and flipped the breakers, one, two, three, four.

An electronic lock needs power. When the electricity is cut off, some models will open automatically. Some will lock and stay locked until the company opens it. Others have battery backup. I couldn't tell which model Ty Collins had. This was a chance I had to take.

I walked back through the apartment. Lights blinked from the kitchen. The clocks now read 00:01. I'd have to reset them before I left.

I tried the handle of the door to the photo room. It opened toward me. I was inside, alone with the Jane Brick photos.

I took one off the wall and examined the frame. It was difficult to open. It had to be laid flat and the backing eased up. The glass was easy to remove. Then the matte border. Finally I had the photograph.

I plugged in the scanner and carefully fed the photo into the tray, watching as it disappeared into the machine.

While the scanner worked, I took the glass from the frame to the kitchen table. I gently set down the pane of glass I'd brought with me, careful to touch only the edges. I laid the frame glass on top and traced around it. Then I used my glass cutter to cut out a perfect matching rectangle.

I put this new piece of glass in the frame. I'll explain why later.

The scanner was finished. It had printed out a perfect copy of Jane Brick's image. I placed the matte around it and put the frame back together.

It had taken me eleven minutes, but most of that time had been spent measuring and cutting glass. The next photograph took seven minutes. The third took five and a half. At this rate I would be done all ten in an hour. Maybe in forty-five minutes.

Exactly twelve minutes later, I heard the first sirens.

TEN

THE WINDOW IN the living room was open a crack. Sound from the street carried up. Looking down, I saw flashing blue and red lights. Beyond them, the beach and the dark ocean.

The sirens probably had nothing to do with me. But, just in case, I'd go soon.

I finished scanning the fourth photo, put it in the pocket of the nylon case and set the copy in the frame. Once it was back on the wall, I packed up. The pane of glass had been cut into even rectangles. I packed the leftovers into the bag, along with the glass from the frames, and the scanner. Lastly, I reset the clocks on the stove and microwave.

A buzzer went off, loud in the quiet apartment. A doorbell, I guessed. The monitor on the wall glowed. On the screen two police officers stared at the camera and into the front entrance of the building. One of them was Phil Kushida. I made sure to stand to the side, away from the camera's eye.

"Mr. Collins?" Phil said. "We're with the police. We believe someone is planning on robbing you. Would you let us in?"

I had planned to walk out the front entrance of the building and drive away, but that was impossible now. I needed a new exit. I was glad I hadn't left anything important in the van.

Maybe the back or side entrance? It was a large building. There was always the parking garage, two floors below ground, but it required a different key and an electronic gate opener. If I couldn't pick the lock before the police found me, I'd be trapped.

I pushed open the living room window. It was four feet tall and almost too narrow to crawl through. Almost. Looking up, the roof was eight feet above me. The surface between here and there was glass. I had a small amount of rope, but nothing to tie it to.

Looking down made me sick. I stopped looking down.

There was movement on the monitor. Phil and the other officer were stepping through the entrance. Maybe another tenant had buzzed them in, or they'd talked to the landlord or the security company. However they'd done it, they were on their way. I had to move faster.

If the window had faced east instead of west, I could have tried to climb to the roof of the building next door. It was close and about the same size. But there was nothing outside and no way to swing around.

I slung the bag across my shoulder. Climbing up onto the windowsill, I opened the window as far as it would go. The breeze hit me like a cold wave. I could smell salt water from the ocean.

Don't look down, I told myself. Just don't.

As the window swung open, I held on to the top edge and stepped onto the handle. I climbed up the piece of glass so that my feet were balanced on its edge. The window swung out above the street. Above my head was the edge of the roof.

Like standing on a wire, I thought. The glass swung closed a little bit. I didn't breathe.

As careful as a bomb technician, I raised my hands over my head. The edge was just above my fingers. I'd have one shot at this. I would count to three.

One.

Don't look down.

Two.

Loud knocking from the door to the apartment. The doorknob rattled.

The lock turned.

Had I left anything inside? No way.

Don't think about it. Don't think about anything.

Concentrate.

Don't look down.

Three.

I jumped.

It was a small jump, but I was able to grab on to the rough surface of the roof, and with all my might I pulled, pulled, crawled my way up. The window swung closed. I rolled away from the edge.

I looked up at a full yellow moon, just out of reach, and a million bright stars. Nothing had ever looked better.

When I had recovered, I walked to the other end of the roof. The building next to this one was older. A fire escape hung down the side, a maze of ladders and stairs. I slung the bag across my shoulder and made my second risky jump of the night.

I climbed quickly down the zigzag of stairs. At the bottom of the fire escape I jumped to the alley. A short, simple jump, but I felt a jolt of pain in my left leg.

In the alley I took off the uniform and threw it away. Then I headed to the pawn-shop to meet Lisa. I had only four of the ten photos. It would have to be enough.

ELEVEN

I STEPPED OFF the bus a block from Lisa's pawn-shop. All the stores were closed for the night. The streets were empty. Some of the street-lights had burned out. I knew how they felt.

It was dark inside the Silver Lode. I knocked on the door. There was no movement inside. I waited and knocked again.

Behind me I heard the purr of an engine. Lisa was sitting behind the wheel of an expensive-looking truck with black windows.

"Change of venue," she said. "Let's do this at Kidd's."

I climbed into the passenger seat and set my bag on the floor behind me. "Nice car," I said.

"It beats riding the bus, doesn't it?"

"I like the bus."

Lisa laughed. "Of course you do, Ali. You've always been cheap. You could've made so much more money if you'd treated yourself better."

"I treat myself fine, Lisa. And there's always a cost for nice things."

"Whatever. Do you have the photos?"

"Some of them."

"Where are the rest?"

"Still in their cases."

"So you didn't complete the job."

"You never expected me to," I said.

Lisa stared straight ahead, but a smile crept over the corners of her mouth. "What could you possibly mean?" she said.

"I mean the police showed up. And I don't know if you sent them there or if they were onto the job some other way. I wasn't in the place that long before they were."

"But you got away," Lisa said. "How did you do it? It's impossible to climb out of there, isn't it?"

"I never reveal my secrets," I said.

Lisa parked behind the restaurant. It was almost closing time. There were only a few customers inside. One of them was Max. A cup and an empty pot of coffee sat on the counter in front of him.

"He's been here for three hours," Dean said to me. "Coffee only. He didn't even order dessert."

"He hasn't done anything, has he?"

"Just sat there," Dean said.

I hugged Dean and told him it was good to see him. "I need to talk to Lisa in the back. After that I'll help you clean up, okay?"

Dean nodded and went back to wiping down the counter.

In the office I put the case down on the desk. Lisa pushed me aside. She opened it and took out the photos, which were sitting at the very top of the case.

"Excellent work," she said, holding them up to the light to make sure they were real. "This might even be better than having all ten. The art gallery will want the full set. They'll probably pay a fortune for these."

"Why did the police get to Collins's place so quickly?" I asked.

"They knew I wanted the photos," Lisa said, still staring at them. "Max tried to get them for me once before. The building security thought he was just a hockey fan who wanted an autograph. But that cop Kushida, he knows Max works for me."

"You didn't tell me the police were watching," I said.

"You didn't need to know that, Ali."

I changed into a white kitchen smock and put a white cap on my head. Lisa zipped up the case.

"We had a deal," I said. "You leave Dean and me alone. Right?"

"Ali, I would never hurt your brother. And I'd never ask you to do something you didn't secretly want to. Admit it. You enjoyed this, didn't you?"

I said nothing. My leg hurt, I felt beyond tired, and I was still worried that Phil had caught a glimpse of me in the apartment on the security camera at Ty's apartment. But I did feel alive. I hated to admit that she was right.

"I won't need to bother you again," Lisa said. "You'll come to me. You can put on all the kitchen whites you want, Ali, but you're a born thief. You'll always be a thief. And you'll always need someone like me."

She left. I helped Dean mop the floor and

clean the grill. As I did I wondered how right Lisa was. Could I really give up something I was so good at, something I enjoyed?

I guessed I'd have to find out.

> ◆ <

An hour after closing, the restaurant was spotless. Dean was adding up the day's receipts in his office. I put away the last load of dishes. There was a knock on the door so loud that it nearly made me break a plate.

I fixed my hair under the cap before unlocking the door.

"Any chance of a last-minute coffee?" Phil Kushida asked.

I poured what was left into a takeaway cup. "Busy night?"

"Pretty busy, yeah. A few hours ago someone broke into the home of Ty Collins. He's a hockey player."

"I don't watch much hockey," I said.

"Ty collects photos. Have you heard of Jane Brick? He owns some rare photos of hers. They're worth a lot of money."

"How can a photo be worth money?" I asked. "Can't you just make another one with the...what do you call it? The negative?"

"If you have the negative," Phil said. "These are one of a kind. Probably worth at least a million."

I whistled. "That's a lot."

"Someone tried to steal them tonight."

"Tried to?" I said.

"Looks like we got there in time. The thief ran away. Climbed away, more like it. You won't believe it. He or she climbed from the thirtieth floor to the roof."

"Crazy," I said. "Did you catch him?"

Phil looked closely at me. "I have an idea who he is. Or she. The security footage at the door shows someone dressed as a window-repair person. A witness says she saw a woman in the alley next door."

My heartbeat had tripled. I tried to look casual and kept putting away cups and plates.

"The witness only caught a glimpse of our thief," Phil said. "She says the person has silver hair. Do you know anyone like that? A woman with silver hair who could climb a building like that? Or maybe a woman with hair dyed silver?"

I stopped. He was going to ask me to take off the kitchen cap. He'd see my hair. That would be it.

Phil pointed at my shirt and cap. "That uniform," he said. "It's a good fit on you."

"Thanks," I said, stunned.

"Thank you for the coffee, Ali. Stay out of trouble."

"You too," I said. But the door was already closing. Phil waved goodbye.

TWELVE

THREE WEEKS LATER I saw Phil again. He came to the restaurant at five in the morning, before we opened. Salmon was on the dinner menu, and Dean was showing me how to fillet the fish.

"It's just like this," he said, holding the tail and gently running his knife along the fish, under the skin. A silver ribbon peeled off, leaving red meat with white marbles running through it. Five quick cuts and the fish was in equal portions. "Simple, right? Now you try, Ali."

By the time I was finished, my fish looked more like spaghetti. I had scales on my hands and arms, even on my cheeks.

"Sorry," I said.

"It's all right. We can do fish stew tomorrow."

That was when I heard the knocking. I quickly washed my hands and opened the door to Phil. I'd dyed my hair back to its natural color and destroyed all the evidence of what I'd done. But I still felt slightly nervous, talking with a cop. Even a friendly cop.

"Not causing anyone trouble, I hope?" he asked.

"That depends on if you ask any fish."

He sat down. "I have some news that might interest you. Remember when I said someone tried to steal photos from Ty Collins?"

"Sure."

"Well, it turns out they did steal some. Four of them turned out to be fakes."

"That's too bad," I said.

"We know who did it too."

I waited.

"The thief thought she was smart," Phil said. "But they all make mistakes. It's the little details that catch up to you eventually."

"To me?" I asked.

"I mean to anyone. In the case of our thief, it was fingerprints. She thought she had been careful, but when we dusted the glass inside the frames of the photos, we found her prints."

"Maybe she just visited the apartment," I said. "As a guest. Maybe she looked at the photos."

"Not possible," Phil said. "The finger-prints were on the inside surface of the glass, in the frame."

"Damn."

"Damn is right. From there we got a warrant for her home and her place of business."

"So why are you here?" I asked.

"I just needed a coffee," Phil said. "We spent all night searching Lisa Wan's pawnshop, her house, even her car. We found the photos in the pawnshop safe. On the counter was a printer-scanner thing that was probably used to make the copies. And under the seat of her car we found a key to Ty Collins's door. She says she doesn't know how it got there. Is there any chance, Ali?"

"Any chance of what?" I asked.

"Any chance of that coffee."

I smiled at him. "I'll put some on," I said.

As the coffee brewed, Phil told me that Lisa was claiming to be innocent, but the police had found enough stolen goods in the pawnshop to get another warrant. She would probably be going away for a long time.

"Her associate, Max Smith. He'll be going away too. Do you know him?"

"I've seen them together," I said.

"A lot of people close to Lisa Wan have gone to jail. Not her though. Not till now."

"Guess everyone's luck runs out," I said.

The coffee was ready. I poured two cups, then added cream and sugar to Phil's.

"I have to ask this, Ali. If you don't want to answer, you don't have to."

"Go ahead."

"Lisa says she was framed. Do you think there's any truth to that?"

"How could there be?" I said.

"That's not an answer."

I looked at my cup, then back at Phil. His expression was gentle. Patient.

"Think about it logically," I said. "You know Lisa deals in stolen stuff. You told me her prints were inside the glass of the forgeries in Ty's apartment. And you found the photos in her safe."

"All true," Phil said.

"What's more likely—that she broke in and took them, or that some other person broke in for her, gave her the photos and planted evidence to frame her?"

"Maybe that other person felt threatened," Phil said. "Maybe she didn't feel she had a choice."

"Maybe. But she—or he—would have had to somehow get Lisa's fingerprints on the glass inside the frames. Wouldn't that mean they had to carry around a piece of glass that Lisa had touched and then cut pieces to fit the frames? Is that even possible?"

"If that person was desperate, maybe."

"But it's hard to believe," I said. "To do that, you'd have to be really smart. And feel really threatened."

Phil sipped his coffee, closed his eyes and let out a sigh of satisfaction. "Best dark roast in the city. I should come here more often."

"Any time," I said.

It was five thirty. Time to open up. I flipped the sign in the window from *SORRY—WE'RE CLOSED* to *WELCOME— WE'RE OPEN*! I handed Phil a menu, but he knew what he wanted. Eggs over easy, bacon and sausage, black pudding, brown toast and silver-dollar pancakes. A newspaper. And a lot more coffee.

Dean had finished the fish and was heating the grill. I handed him Phil's order. "That's a lot for a small guy," he said, cracking the eggs with one hand. He began to hum as he cooked.

Two more customers arrived. I took their orders. When I brought Phil his food, he pointed to something in the newspaper.

"New exhibition at the art gallery," he said. "Rare impressionist masterpieces on loan from the Musée d'Orsay in Paris. What do you think?"

"Security will be tight," I said. "Difficult but definitely not impossible."

"I meant what do you think about going there?" He blushed. "With me."

"Oh. Sure," I said. "I like art."

"Just to look at, right?"

I shook my head. "How can you ask that, Phil? I'm 100 percent retired."

"Then I'll pick you up after work," he said. "Is six o'clock all right?"

I was thinking about the gallery. The way to do it would be from inside. Get hired by the security company, maybe using fake identification. Wait until closing time, when people were leaving all together. Maybe arrange for an alarm to go off in a different room. In all that confusion, would anyone notice?

Phil caught my look. He folded up the paper. "You really meant it, didn't you, Ali? About being retired? One hundred percent?"

I shrugged. "Let's start with 99.9 percent and see how it goes."

ACKNOWLEDGMENTS

Special thanks to Ruth Linka, Vivian Sinclair, Olivia Gutjahr, and the people at Orca for their editorial guidance; to copyeditor Sarah Weber; to Andrew Nicholls for the info on security codes; to my mom, Linda, and brothers Dan and Josh; and to Dieter, Linda and everyone in the Vancouver crime writing community.

SAM WIEBE is the award-winning author of the Vancouver crime novels *Cut You Down*, *Invisible Dead* and *Last of the Independents*. His short stories have appeared in *Thuglit*, *Spinetingler* and *subTerrain*. He is a former Vancouver Public Library Writer in Residence and the winner of the 2015 Kobo Emerging Writer Prize. Sam lives in Vancouver.